ALMINGTON ACADEMY

MOROTI OYEYEMI

1

Arriving at the beginning

"Are you excited, Joey?" my mom asked from the passenger seat.

"Why would I be? You are shipping me off to boarding school," I replied.

"Joseph, respect your mother. That's part of the reason we're 'shipping you off.' And don't forget that you could've prevented this," my stepdad replied for her.

"Brad, you've been talking about doing this with mom since I was in sixth grade. You waited for me to slip up just once, so you could send me away for good."

My stepdad, Brad, pulled over and turned around to say, "you should be happy. You're going to Almington Academy, the best high school in the nation. They're the best in everything academic and sports. We'll call you every day and visit you once a month."

He started driving again, I chose not to respond. Thirty minutes of silence later, we arrived at a street named Almington Avenue. My mom turned to me and flashed a petty smile.

The campus was ginormous. It was like a major city, expansive, well-built gardens, beautiful old and modern architecture, great network of roads, good transportation, clean, calm and pristine environment.

My sister, sitting next to me, in the back seat, gazed in awe, we were amazed by the stunning and captivating reality of Almington Academy.

About five minutes later, we arrived at a huge parking lot in front of a small building.

A sign at the front read "Drop-Off". My stepdad smiled at the sight of the building and parked. When it was time for me to get out, Brad said, "enjoy, see you in a month." I didn't respond.

I slammed the door behind me and walked to the other side of the car where Elizabeth, my sister, was seated behind my mom. Elizabeth rolled down her window, removed her sunglasses and said, "I'll miss you, bro, see you in a few weeks. Call me if you need anything." I smiled and hugged her through the window.

My sister and I never got along until our parents got divorced, and Brad came into our lives. We both did not like him and the way our mom looked at him with heart-eyes all the time. I saw my stepdad sneer in the background, I turned away.

My mom stepped out with a wry smile and gestured for us to walk toward the building. We'd been instructed not to bring anything from home, to the school, because they were going to provide us with everything that we needed.

We arrived inside the building after a short walk and were met by a tall, young guy with huge shoulders and brown hair. My mom did all the sign-in stuff, I was led into another room, after I said bye to my mom.

In the back, I was given a maroon shirt to put on, with two white stripes on the collar. I walked to the dressing room and changed, into the khaki shorts that I was provided. When I got out, a camera stand with a white screen background was already set up. I stood in front of the backdrop, and my picture was taken.

In a matter of seconds, I looked over to the small, loud machine that was printing some type of card. The tall guy gestured toward the machine, so I walked over and picked up the card that read, "Joseph Hardester: Age: 15 - Class of 2018," with a pretty crappy picture of me on it.

"You can walk out that door and get on Bus 05. It'll take you to your dorm," said the guy while pointing at a door at the back of the little shack.

After I got on the bus, I noticed a group of about twenty - three other boys who all had similar looks on their faces, like it was their first day in prison. There was one kid in the back, he seemed to be staring out the window at another bus on the other side of the parking lot. He was so happy that he appeared to be drooling in his seat.

All the buses I'd seen were maroon, but these other ones were burgundy. There was a much bigger difference, which is why he was staring at them, girls were boarding the other buses.

"Are you ready for this school year?" the weird kid asked, I nodded.

The bus driver came on the intercom and yelled, "everyone, have a seat!"

I turned to the seat I was previously planning to sit in but, to my surprise, the whole bus was filled with two people to a seat, except one; the seat next to the weird kid. I sat beside him, and he continued to stare at the buses with the girls, as our bus pulled out of the parking lot.

We began our journey into the main campus, along the way, the bus driver started giving a tour; "my name is Jim Closefield, welcome to Almington Academy. Most people call the school by its short name; AA. This school amazes me every day. Your dorm custodians will give you a more detailed tour tomorrow, this is merely a mini tour."

I ignored everything else the bus driver said, I

was admiring the huge campus with towering skyscrapers. They all had weird names like "Almanack Hall" and "Improvisation Chamber." There was one building with an inscription; "Migglamizzule" on the huge front cathedral doors, it stuck out to me more than the other the other buildings. It was the tallest by far and had 12 giant statures.

"That's where they execute the bad kids," the boy seating beside me said. I turned to look at him, my face expressed my shock.

"Hi kid, I kid", he added.

I sighed in relief. Then he said, "are you mute? If you are, I mean, that's okay too. No offense. I was, uh, just wondering." Then he looked out the window as his face turned red.

"Nah, bro," I replied with a small laugh.

"Oh, ha-ha," he replied, we both looked out the window, our jaws dropped at the sight of more imposing buildings.

A series of buildings lined the street. "We have five corners here at AA. There are two corners of dorms. The boys' corner, Merribridge, and the girls' corner, Violetcliff."

Then whispers floated through the bus. Most of our parents had told us that this was an all-boys school. "Another is the research corner; Van Perrel, which is where your teachers spend most of their time, they all have offices there. There are barely any classes there, in fact, you'd be lucky to get one on your schedule. Van Perrel has twenty-two facilities, it's one of the bigger corners.

Summerfort is another corner, it's the career corner. It has twenty-five facilities, including the Grand Perriman Parlor; that's the library and Space Program Institute – SPI. A little further away, we have the AA Hospital, which would be on your left."

The buildings were huge, I clearly didn't imagine buildings like this in a high school.

Mr. Closefield – our driver, continued calling out buildings as we drove through Summerfort. Then we started driving in what seemed like a circle. We went through a tunnel, looked up and saw fields as far as the eye could see, with a single road that branched out to each field. On the main road, which the bus driver was driving through, there was a huge facility.

"Welcome to the athletics corner, which we call Hollowvale. That building we're headed toward is called the P.E Chamber, it's the biggest facility on campus. Inside the "P.E Chamber", we have multiple swimming pools, tennis courts, basketball courts, and indoor fields. And a lot more," he stated.

Mr. Closefield continued; "within the athletics corner, on the other side of the P.E. Chamber, we have our twenty-five-seat capacity hall, used for conferences, graduation ceremonies and musical, business and trade shows, it's called Hollowvale Hall."

We went through a roundabout, came back out

the exit, and made our way from Hollowvale.

"Now I've given you an impromptu tour of the five corners. Any questions?" asked Mr. Closefield.

"When so we get a full tour?" asked a kid with freckles, in the front seat. "Good question. Your IDs have a magnetic chip inside of them, which are used to access different parts of AA. All of you on this bus only have clearance to Merribridge until you get your schedules. I only have access to Merribridge as well, so you're not alone," he answered.

The bus pulled up to a huge gate that had five skyscrapers, each about forty-six stories high. They formed a circle around a large park, with a single building in the middle. The building was six stories high.

The gate had an inscription; "MB" in a bold, golden print. The security guard at the gate, exchanged a few words with Mr. Closefield, both men laughed, as the huge black gates opened.

Mr. Closefield then pulled the bus over, stood up and said; "thank you for riding the Alligator Express. Walk through the gate, and your dorm custodian will be waiting for you.

You are all Group 5, so the man standing over there, in black, is going to be your custodian this semester". As he concluded, he gestured to a muscular young man who looked like a college student. He was the tallest of all the young-looking custodians, all wearing black pants and T-shirts. We got off the bus and met with him.

2

The tidal force of the sky suite

"Hello, everyone. My name is Christian, but you can call me Chris. I graduated from AA six years ago, I am your dorm custodian. You are all going to be in building 5. Most of you are on levels two to forty-four, except for......" Chris stated, before reaching into his back pocket for a wrinkled piece of paper. Then he read, "Joseph Hardester. But I presume you go as Joey, right?"

I was surprised, I stared at him, looked around to see that all eyes were me. "Uh, yeah. I do," I replied with a subtle stutter.

"Well, you have the Sky Suite on levels forty-five and forty-six. That's a blessing and a curse," he said, turning with a smirk. I furrowed my eyebrows and looked back down at my feet as my ears picked the suppressed whispers of the other students. As we started walking through the park to building five, I turned around to see other students getting off their buses.

After we scanned our IDs at the door, we all met in the lobby. Chris walked up to the front desk and picked up a stack of papers. He sifted through them, mumbled something, began calling names and handing everyone a piece of paper.

He finally got to me. My paper was blue color instead of white. When I retrieved my paper, I asked, "what did you mean by my room is a blessing and a curse?"

"Well you have one a great accommodation on campus but your roommate…" he replied with a grin.

"What about him?"

"He is not the serious type. No one can tell if he is here to study or to party," replied Chris, motioning to one of the five elevators.

All the other students were lined up to get into the other four elevators, but this one had a golden circle around the letters, "SS" written in bold black print.

I entered the elevator and Chris followed. We stood there alone, then he told me to swipe my ID. I followed his directions; I placed my ID on the black sensor pad and the door began to close. I heard the whispers of the kids who were in line.

"Is there a button I'm supposed to press?" I enquired.

"Press that button for a surprise," replied Chris.

I hesitated and he snickered. As soon as I pressed it, the walls and the floor of the elevator appeared to turn into glass, changing from the golden color it was. I could instantly see a great view of AA; the skyline, intriguing architecture, breathtaking landscape, alluring gardens, buses, cars, the network of roads, cascading waterfalls and people at different spots. It was such a beauty to see from that vantage point.

"You'll love it here, especially as you will be staying in the Sky Suite," Chris stated, as the elevator came to a slow halt. "That's your suite, Joey", Chris said pointing to the opaque glass door. "Be downstairs at five for orientation." he yelled as he left. I heard Chris go back down on the elevator, behind me. I placed my ID on the door sensor pad, it crisply opened to reveal an awe-inspiring sight.

The outer walls of the suite were glass and had a brilliant view of AA. The suite was very spacious, a family of eight could live comfortably in it, I thought. I walked around and saw two fully stocked refrigerators on opposite sides. The fridges had two huge LED screens on each of them. There was a breakfast bar made of golden granite, right in the center, between the two fridges. The lower level was painted white with maroon accents. There was a pool table, surrounded by lounge chairs. There were four TVs, hung on the walls around the pool table, visible from all sides.

I looked straight to the right and there was a stairwell; a few steps up and I was on the upper level. I immediately noticed a diamond-encrusted, maroon door, which I opened, it led to a study.

A study with two desktop computers and two large monitors, a laptop, a digital fireplace, and a curved sixty-two-inch television. There was a trash can and shredder in the corner of the study.

I exited the room and walked out, on to the balcony; "what!" I exclaimed, "a swimming pool balcony?" I yelled out loud, I could not contain it, it blew my mind. Right across the landing was a glass bottomed infinity pool. It had high glass railing. It was scary, tempting, yet peaceful. I stood there mesmerized, it was priceless, just being there.

I was startled by an odd voice that echoed from behind me.

"Pretty tight, eh?" said the tall boy with messy, blond hair and deep-blue eyes.

He looked like a guy who threw parties all day and night and wasn't here for the scholastic aspect of it. He was wearing maroon pajamas. My conclusion about this rather rough looking guy, was drawn from the description Chris gave me, his appearance merely confirmed it.

"Yeah! Who are you?" I replied.

"Your roommate, obviously."

"Do you have a name?"

"Ken."

"Well, hi, Ken."

"Yup, I'm your textbook rich kid," he said as he reached toward a small box that looked like it controlled the hot tub. The box contained two buttons, one was black, the other was red.

"Wanna see something cool?" he asked.

"Sure?" I replied.

Ken pressed the black button and the high glass railing that surrounded the balcony rose up and bent over, to one side, creating a roof over the swimming pool balcony. The floor-lights came on to reveal a midnight paradise. I stood there in astonishment. Ken pressed the red button and the dome-like roof retracted.

I was startled yet again by a loud buzz. "There is someone at the door", Ken said.

He walked inside, I followed him. He reached for his phone, looked at it, shook his head in disgust and said to me; "if you thought I was bad, just wait for these two."

His phone was on speaker, so I heard someone yell; "open up, Kenneth." Ken didn't reply, he went down the stairs to the lower level, opened the door and let in two guys.

The two guys were the same height, one had a bottle of what looked like vodka.

"Whassup, dummies!" yelled the blond guy who had to be Ken reincarnate. He looked exactly like Ken except a little taller and well groomed. The other guy had wavy, brown hair that flowed backwards and green eyes.

"Joey meet Keefe. Keefe meet Joey, my new roommate," said Ken.

"Sup," I said, trying to be as chill as possible.

Keefe slung his arm around Ken and made his hair even messier by rubbing it around and saying, "If you haven't noticed, this is my little bro."

The expression on Ken's face made me laugh a little.

"Sup, man. I'm Glenn. Glenn West," said the brown-haired boy as he approached me with his hand out.

"Sup," I replied, shaking his hand.

Then he reached into his pocket and said, with a wink, "in celebration of the newest addition to the Boy's Pinnacle Club, I say we throw a banger."

Ken rolled his eyes as he said, "I have orientation in three hours, and I think I wanna get some sleep."

"Joey, I'll show you to your room. Keefe and Glenn, let yourselves out," Ken said.

With that, Ken led me back into the luxurious suite as Glenn yelled out, "party at your place tonight! Woo!"

Ken didn't acknowledge them. He led me back to the upper level, to another section of the floor, through a glass door with aluminum panel frame. Pointing to the right side with a door that had "Room 2" on it; he said, "that's your room, mine is to the left".

He proceeded to press the glittering black button on the door to reveal my new room.

Once the door opened, it exposed a circular room surrounded with darkening-glass panels. The bed was in the exact middle of the room, there was a mini lounge in the room.

I jumped onto the bed. Ken let himself out after about ten seconds of me lying on the very comfortable bed.

I felt sleepy but before I could, Ken came storming into my room, "do you have a phone?" he asked.

"No."

"Get something to wear from your closet and meet me downstairs in five.

Ken left as I struggled to find the closet. After about two minutes, a small sliding glass door which blended in with the lounge, caught my attention. I pushed it open to find several identical collared shirts.

They were exactly like the one I was wearing—maroon, polo-type shirts with two white stripes on the collar. The only two options for pants were khaki shorts and long pants.

Farther in the closet, I found a selection of pull-over sweaters, sweatshirts, and quarter zips. They all had two stripes on them somewhere. To the left of the deep closet, there was a maroon swimsuit under a selection of T-shirts and long sleeve white shirts. I also found maroon pajamas, like the one Ken wore earlier.

I quickly wore a T-shirt and slipped into a pair of khaki shorts. I wore white socks and slipped into one of the four khaki-colored Sperry boat shoes that were placed at the bottom of the closet. I left to meet Ken downstairs.

He was on the phone with someone but hung up as soon as I came down. He was wearing a collared shirt and khaki shorts. His collar was flared and had three stripes on it.

"What's with the stripes?" I asked him.

"It represents grades: one for freshman, two for sophomore, three for juniors and four for seniors," he replied.

It was then that I noticed he was a junior, and his brother and Glenn were both seniors.

"Let's go; we're late," Ken said, heading to the elevator door. I followed him, and we went down the elevator to the lobby. We exited the large glass doors and made a loop to the back of the building. We walked into a concrete parking garage where many luxurious cars were parked.

Ken and I walked toward a sleek, jet black car, he reached into his pocket, brought out a metallic silver card and pointed toward the black car.

Immediately, the car pulled out of its parking spot and rolled up to him. I witnessed in shock as I headed to the passenger side, wondering what was happening. The door opened by itself in a scissor formation, I nervously got into the car and gleefully sat inside the luxurious sedan car.

"Did Mr. Closefield give you a tour already?" asked Ken.

"Yeah, a mini tour, he called it," I replied, still shocked about what I had just experienced.

Ken pressed a red button on the ceiling of his car, and the floor beneath us started to move.

I reached up to grab a safety bar, but there was none. Then I realized the car had no seat belts. The floor beneath us descended vertically toward the ground. Once on the ground, Ken accelerated off the metal pad that had brought us down.

We rolled onto a narrow road, he then pressed a button on the center console, an eighteen-inch display appeared between the wheel and the glove compartment.

"Is there a seat belt?" I asked.

"Sure, this car is the latest Mercedes-Maybach Z880. Once the self-drive mode is engaged, the seat belts are triggered to strap the driver and passengers when the car senses possible impact or collision, just relax, you are safer here than out there"; Ken said, to drown my curiosity and nervousness.

"Where are we going?" I questioned.

"Inner AA. Where all the fun is. It's like a mini city."

Suddenly, my seat does a one hundred- and eighty-degrees spin, so did Ken's seat. We turned to face a little space, like a mini living room, the windows went black after Ken's double-clapped cue.

The ceiling lights all came on, revealing two Sahara beige leather seats opposite us, and a crystal black screen in the middle, between our seat and the two seats, opposite us.

Ken clapped once; the crystal black box revealed a flat screen that could be watched from both sides. He said, "Channel 8", voice activating the TV, to show us channel 8. Netflix began to play on the screen, Ken reclined his seat and began to watch.

I was spellbound by the transformation; it was dreamlike but real. We both began to watch a reality TV show about zookeepers called Love and Living Animals.

It was a stupid show, but it certainly kept us laughing.

"When are we gonna leave, man?" I demanded.

"Oh crap!" Ken exclaimed while he spun us back

around and pressed a blue button that opened the front doors of the car. They opened to expose a large outlet, complete with every type of store except clothing. I had no idea we'd been sitting in the parking lot for almost an hour. I stepped out, Ken locked his car, using metallic silver card and gestured for me to follow him. We were parked right in front of an Apple store.

We walked through a revolving glass door, into the Apple store. The store had three floors; the ground floor was for phones and accessories, the middle floor for MacBooks, and the top floor was a service center. Ken went straight to a guy with a name tag that read; Tony – Store Manager. They greeted and Ken said to him; "we'll take two of the newest iPhones."

The manager opened the cabinet next to him, grabbed tow iPhones 12XG, and handed them over to Ken. His ID was scanned, he said, "thanks Tony" and we left the store. When we got back into the car, Ken gave me one of the phones and said; "use the phone to scan your ID and all of your stuffs will sync."

I did as Ken instructed, I scanned my ID and all the photos from my old phone transferred over, but my contact list had only twenty-nine names and phone numbers, of people I could not recognize. I leaned over to Ken and showed him the contacts list on my phone.

"Those are all the students that have a Sky Suite

and Chris, our dorm custodian," Ken stated.

"Where are you here?" I inquired, Ken pointed to a name that read, Kenneth Hollowvale.

"Waaiiittt," I started, before I was interrupted by a haughty sigh from Ken.

"My great-grandfather and two other families founded Almington Academy. The Summerforts and the Almingtons."

"Bro, that explains why you are so rich?" I exclaimed.

"What do you mean? You're obviously as 'rich' as I am."

"How?" I asked.

"You're staying in the Sky Suite. Two hundred fifty thousand dollars a semester. With the Pinnacle status. That's upwards of three hundred and fifty thousand dollars a semester. If you add it all up, you'd be staying here on a price tag of 2.1 million dollars by the time you graduate."

I was shocked at Ken's tuition calculation, knowing that there was no way my parents could afford that kind of money for my high school education.

We got back to Merribridge. I checked the time on my phone, it was 6:42 p.m. I'd missed the orientation. Soon after my realization, a fleet of students entered the lobby behind Chris.

"Joey! I didn't see you at the orientation," exclaimed Chris with a curious look on his face.

"He was out with me. I gave him a little personal tour," said Ken, gesturing at the shopping bags.

"Well, while you guys were out, I had your new class schedules placed in your rooms," Chris said as he seemed unwilling to engage in a conversation with Ken.

"Can I talk to you, Joey?" Chris asked in a soft whisper. "In private," he continued.

Chris led me to a corner of the lobby, away from Ken and all the other students.

"I'm not saying you shouldn't be friends with your roommate, but I am saying you shouldn't engage in the Pinnacle status activities."

"What does that mean?"

"The Pinnacle class students always throw parties and drink; nobody can ever get them in trouble because they have extremely rich parents. It's easy to get sucked in, and I know you're better than that."

"Thanks for the tip," I said, as I turned to look at Ken, who was obviously listening in on our conversation.

"How do you know all this?" I questioned.

"I know Ken, too well. He and his brother are wild. They constantly throw parties and have no respect for anyone else."

"I mean; they do whatever they want since their family basically invented this place?"

"What's your last name?" I demanded.

"It doesn't matter. Go to your room, review your schedule, and get some rest."

With that, I left and met up with Ken in the elevator. We ascended to our suite in dead silence. When we got upstairs Ken said, "follow me."

I followed him to his room, he led me to his closet and handed me some items that looked extremely exclusive: one diamond studded Rolex, one sapphire Cartier wristwatch and some designer clothes.

"These are for the parties. If you wear your uniform, you'll definitely look stupid."

"Nah, man. I think I'll pass. I'm gonna try and keep a low profile for some time," I replied, returning the clothes to him.

"Consider yourself warned," Ken replied while hanging the clothes back up.

"I'm having a few friends over tonight, we're gonna be in the hot tub. You're always invited to a Hollowvale get-together," Ken stated with a wink.

"Thanks, but I'm a bit tired, I think I'll get an early night," I responded.

I instantly dashed out of his room. I went into my room and proceeded to download a boatload of games. I couldn't resist, with a terabyte of storage. After what seemed like an hour of gaming, I went to the lounge to set up my AA Gaming account. I then played lacrosse video game, for another hour.

Tired, I went to my room to catch a nap, on the

table in my room was my class schedule. I picked the white paper up to see my classes, it read:

- *Period 1A: Zoology -*
  Animal Science Building. [5]. 9–11:30
- *Period 2A: English 101 -*
  Literary Development Building. [4]. 12–1:30
- *Period 3A: Computer Science -*
  Technology Building. [2]. 2–3:30
- *Period 1B: P.E.*
  Physical Education Chamber. [3]. 9–11:30
- *Period 2B: American Government -*
  Social Studies Building. [8]. 12–1:30
- *Period 3B: Algebra 2 - Mathematics Building. [9]. 2–3:30*

Note: Classes start tomorrow!

I lay down on my bed, questioning the zoology part of the schedule, and fell asleep shortly after.

3

Classes with Class

I woke up the next morning to Ken's face at my doorway. He was wearing a maroon shirt with three stripes on the collar, along with khaki shorts. "Hurry up and meet me in the lobby." He said and exited, walking down the stairs. I proceeded to the shower, got dressed, and got on the elevator. In the lobby, I saw Ken talking to Chris about something serious. Once I started walking toward them, they stopped talking, and Chris walked away.

"What was that about?" I asked.

"We were discussing transportation for you," Ken started. "I was gonna be giving you rides to and from class, but Chris insisted that you have a personal driver instead."

"Wait, how do other kids get around?" I asked.

"Alligator Express, Light Train, Bikes and Scooters."

"Then I'll just use that," I stated. Ken rolled his eyes and pulled me closer.

"Joey, we aren't like other students, if you want to fit in, you'll have to learn that."

Then I heard Chris yell from outside, "Joey, come meet someone. I looked at Ken, as he walked away to where he had parked his car, on the street.

"Joey, meet Brent. He's going to be your driver for this semester, then we'll revisit transportation," Chris said. Brent looked to be in his early sixties, he was muscular and well groomed. His hair was slightly gray but very well kept. He had brown eyes and a polite smile across his face.

I shook his hand, and he opened the door of the car that I hadn't even noticed. It was a crystal white pearl Rolls Royce with golden accents. It had a java brown leather interior I sat quite comfortably with a broad smile that anyone would have noticed.

After a nineteen-minute car ride, I arrived at the drop-off area, I could see the animal science building, just a few steps away.

"I'll be parked here once class is over," Brent said.

"Okay, thank you", I replied Brent, as I exited the car.

As Brent rolled away, I looked around and saw

about twelve male students, clustered around the drop-off area, all with their cellphones, taking pictures and recording stuff.

For a minute, I felt like a celebrity on the red carpet, I waved at them and paced my strides like Shawn Mendes, on the MTV video music awards red carpet.

To my dismay, I was not the center of attraction, I realized that they were all enthralled by the car behind me. I stood back and let them take all the pictures they wanted; of the hot-pink Aston Martin DBZ50 that was approaching the drop-off area.

The car slowly and softly pulled over, as though the passenger was fragile and should be transported with the highest level of care. My attention was now aroused, and I wanted to know who the center of the universe now revolved around.

From the passenger's side, a red-haired girl, delicately, stepped out of the hot-pink Aston Martin DBZ50, she looked straight ahead, and walked into the animal science building, briskly.

While still wondering what all the fuss was about, I noticed some female students, walking toward the animal science building. Their uniforms were white shirt on a burgundy skirt, burgundy bow tie, burgundy jacket, white socks and black shoes. They also had different number of white stripes on jacket collar, based on grade.

The animal science building was a series of connecting buildings. There was a lion statue at the entrance. The building consisted of nine levels; I could almost see inside all of them since the walls were made of glass.

I walked in. There was a huge lobby, with two lines of students, ready for class. I got in line, and the boy in front of me whispered, "you can just go to the front"; for whatever reason, I agreed and proceeded to the front.

"Schedule please," said the lady at the desk. I handed her my schedule and she said, "your classroom is on the fifth floor." There were four elevators, each had a small line of students. I got in the line for the elevator to the fifth floor, shortly after, we all got in, it was a little crowded, it didn't matter, I got to the fifth floor and proceeded to class.

Once I arrived in class, I noticed a different layout than I was used to. The triangular shape of the classroom was somewhat beneficial. The teacher was at the front, and the walls seemed to funnel toward her desk. There were fifteen long desks, even though there were thirty students. The teacher was standing at the front of the class, looking over some papers.

The teacher was a tall man, over six feet. His eyes were blue and seemed to be in his early sixties. He had brownish-gray hair and looked like a generally happy guy. It was also evident that he lifted weights in his younger days. He wore a simple quarter zip that read, "Staff." Once all the students had gotten off the elevator, he instructed us to pair up and choose our seats, as he finished his sentence, I felt an arm grab me from behind, I turned and it was the red-haired girl that was in the hot-pink Aston Martin DBZ50. I noticed she had four stripes on her jacket collar, she's certainly a senior, I concluded.

"Follow me," she said, why not, I thought, I did exactly that. I followed her to the desk in the back, right corner of class. The desks were oddly spaced out, but I didn't mind. I was still at a loss for words on why she had chosen me as her partner.

"Sorry, I just didn't want any of those kids as my partner," she said, gesturing at a group of other students that were now starring at both of us, with their mouths ajar. I giggled and sat in silence until everyone found a seat. The teacher got up from his desk and turned to the chalkboard where he wrote, Mr. Scott's Zoology Class.

"Good morning everyone! I hope you've all gotten settled in and are ready for your first day of class", Mr. Scott said, his expression died with the coldness of the room. "Well, to start, I'll call attendance," he said as he opened a drawer in his desk and pulled out the paper he had recently been looking over. He called out the names of everyone, but the only two that caught my attention were Wyatt Heffler, the weird kid who sat next to me on the bus, and Danielle, the red-haired girl, sitting next to me in class.

When my name was called, I noticed Wyatt

looked back at me. He held his gaze for a few seconds, waiting for me to acknowledge him, which I never did. Once Mr. Scott finished with the attendance, he passed out the syllabus for the semester. We had four units and they were mammals, fish, reptiles, and birds. The class seemed like a pretty simple class, and I already had a good amount of knowledge on animals, so I felt this would be a breeze.

After sitting in the class for an hour and a half just listening to him go on and on about his knowledge of animals and all the research he was working on, the bell rang and a feminine, automated voice came over the intercom to say; "please proceed to your period-two class."

Everyone got up and rushed to the elevator. Behind me came a buzzing familiar voice; "did you know the entire Almington Academy administration is run by robots? I turned around and saw the same short, freckled faced boy I had sat next to on the bus. He wore glasses but a lens was missing.

"What's up with your glasses?" I asked.

"On the way here, my bus hit something, my frames fell, and I stepped on them," he said in a rushed tone. We got out of the elevator and I watched him get in line for his bus to come pick him up.

I wasn't sure what it was about him, but I was intrigued by his personality, so I shouted. "What class do you have next?" He turned and pointed to himself as though to confirm whether I was talking to him or not. I nodded, he ran over to me and said, "I have, uh, let's see." Then he reached into his backpack and said, "English 101". He looked up at me, and I cross-checked my period two with his.

"Same here," I said, I noticed his face glow. "Wanna catch a ride" I asked.

He interrupted me with a loud, "yes!" I looked around to see if anyone else had heard the exclamation. I looked over toward Danielle, who was looking at me in disgust from her car door. She got into her car and it glided away quietly.

I led Wyatt to my chauffeur driven car.

"Who's this?" asked Brent.

"My friend. We have the same class next, so I was just gonna give him a ride there." Brent nodded and smiled at Wyatt. Then he reached over into the glove box and pulled out what looked like a grocery scanner.

"ID, please," Brent demanded. Wyatt reached into his pocket in a hurry and handed it to Brent. Something on Wyatt's ID shocked Brent. Brent let out a small laugh and proceeded to scan the card. For once, Wyatt had nothing to say. He was taking in the opulence of the car's interior; he was so shocked that his eyeballs were bulging to explosion.

"Joey, you're the best friend I've ever had," Wyatt said to me. I was a bit confused because I barely even knew him. Let me get to know him, I thought, so I asked him;

"What's your story?"

Wyatt looked at me and started, "well, my family is probably lower-middle class. When I went to the Goldbrick Annual Wildlife Expo, I ran into an AA scout. The scout was so shocked by how much I knew about AA that he engaged me in a lengthy discussion.

We discussed our common interest in animals, and I showed him my Elementary School report on my phone, that impressed him, and he took my contact details. Months after that I was offered a full bronze scholarship to AA. I accepted, of course. Not the story you've probably heard from others, but that's me. What about you?"

"I don't really have one. My parents sent me here," I replied.

"Oh, so your parents are like super-mega rich?" he asked.

"Not at all. I'm still confused by how they could afford me coming here, but hey, I'm not complaining."

"Interesting. Maybe one of your distant relatives is a descendant of the founders of this school. Probably not. I don't know." Those words went right through my ears, and we sat in silence for most of the ride. Then I noticed a small remote control that had ended up on the car foot mat. I picked it up and pressed the "On" button. Almost instantly, our chairs rotated and faced the windows. The windows went pitch black, and the word "Netflix" appeared over the canvas.

“Cool!” Wyatt exclaimed.

I flipped through, and before I could even find something to watch, Brent turned to us and said, “we’re here. This is as close as I can get to the building, but I think you guys will be fine.” I turned the TVs off as I proceeded to exit the car.

4

Fists of the Pinnacles

As Wyatt and I walked away from the car, I heard someone call my name, I looked back, it was Brent, he rolled down the driver's side window and softly and precisely said; "Joey, just some friendly advice, don't get too involved with students that aren't in your social class. You do that and the people you would call your friends will reject you, that would force you out of your Pinnacle status. Don't do that to yourself, Joey,".

The straight look in his eyes showed how serious he was about what he said. I thanked him, turned to Wyatt, who looked ready to conquer the world. I let

Brent's words really sink in. Can they really force me out of my Pinnacle status just for talking to people like Wyatt? I thought. I shook it off and proceeded to walk toward the Literary Development building with Wyatt.

The Literary Development building was basically a huge glass rectangular structure, it had a golden brick road that was at least a quarter mile long. "The bricks are a Wizard of Oz reference. We all read that book in freshman year," Wyatt said.

"How did you know I wasn't here last year?" I asked him.

He stuttered before saying, "well, don't think I'm weird, but I've been kinda stalking you since you arrived. You just looked like a really nice person, I guess."

I didn't respond. I then asked him, "what class do you have next, after English 101?"

"Um, it says…" he started, reaching into his backpack. "Art. You?"

"Computer Science," I replied.

His boisterous expression faded as he yanked my class schedule from my hands and read through it. "We only have Zoology, English, and Math together, well, three is greater than one," he concluded.

All I could do was stare at him; I was like a spectator in a self-created drama. He continued talking, he muttered some words that were not quite audible. As I was thinking about that, I heard a familiar voice call me. "No way! Is that Joseph? Get over here, bro!". I looked over to see Keefe staring straight at me, gesturing for me to come over.

Wyatt began walking toward them with me, so I told him, "wait here."

As I walked toward Keefe, I realized he was standing with Ken, Glenn, Danielle, and two other female students who I didn't recognize. "What's up?" I said to Keefe.

"Bro, I missed you at the party yesterday! Where were you?" he asked.

"I needed some sleep. I was pretty winded from shopping all day," I replied. Keefe laughed, his laughter was contagious, others began to laugh too; except for Ken, he was not amused at all. He seemed annoyed, either by my presence or by his brother's cockiness.

"It's whatever, man! Meet Danielle, Emily, and Cheyenne," he said, gesturing for me to shake hands with them. While Danielle and Cheyenne both had four stripes on their collar, Emily had just two.

Emily had dark brown hair and green eyes. She had a petite figure, but she looked athletic. She was a few inches shorter than I was, but she wasn't awkwardly short.

Cheyenne was slightly taller than her, they had similar facial features, except Cheyenne had blue eyes and blonde hair. She had a bit more of a muscular build, it wasn't anything over the top. "I've already met him," Danielle said, a bit disgusted. "Why didn't your friend come with you?" she questioned, looking over at Wyatt.

"Hm, I don't recognize him. What building is he in?" Keefe asked.

"Mine," I replied.

"He's a bruin," Danielle stated, before Keefe could put the pieces together. Glenn busted out laughing and Keefe followed. Ken walked away, and Danielle followed him. Cheyenne couldn't help but laugh a little bit, I was embarrassed, so I began walking away. My face grew red, I wasn't sure what she meant by bruin, whatever it meant, it was a not good thing.

I noticed a dark figure appear next to me. It was Emily. "Don't mind them. They're a bit wild," she stated.

"Oh, ha ha, I was just gonna get to class," I said, ignoring how shaky my voice was.

"Yeah, we're in the same class," she said.

"How do you know?"

"Well, I noticed your stripes and you're here, so I just assumed we are in the same class."

"Oh. Do you know what a bruin is?" I inquired.

"Yeah, that's the word they use to make fun of the students in the bronze class. Pinnacles don't really associate with anyone that isn't in their class," she stated.

"Their class? Aren't you in the Pinnacle class too?" I probed.

She smiled and said, "let me explain the social status ranking system at AA to you. The least class; the bottom feeders, the poor, belong to the bronze class. After that, you have students from slightly okay families, they belong to the silver class. The gold class are for students that are kind of there but not there yet".

Emily continued, saying; "to matter here at AA, you must either belong to the Diamond class; which is for students with very rich parents or the extremely exclusive class called pinnacle class – that's the crown jewel. It does not get any better than that, it's the highest level, for the super wealthy students".

"Emily, I know that AA is an extremely socially segregated high school. I also understand the social classifications of bronze, silver, gold, diamond and pinnacle, what I don't get is why students should mock, disgrace and humiliate each other about it.

Think of it, we did not put ourselves in the social class we belong, it's our parents social class, not ours, we should not bear the burden of it or pay the price for it – I might be wrong, but that's my opinion", I stated with some venom.

"You make sense to me but that's the way the world is, who's gonna change it; you?", she demanded.

"Am not taking a bullet for nobody", I jested; she laughed and said, "me neither".

We laughed louder walking toward Wyatt, who was also walking in our direction.

"Wyatt, this is Emily. Emily meet Wyatt." I introduced both, they shook hands, and Wyatt acted normal for once. I felt comfortable around these two, I felt like if I had them with me, I could take the school year, head-on.

The three of us started walking toward the Literary Development building for our English 101 class. "Please proceed to your next class," the voice on intercom yelled out.

I sat next to Wyatt and Emily in class, through the glass wall, I could almost see Violetcliff.

The teacher's name was Mrs. Perez, she looked like she'd been sleeping all day. She had shoulder-length, black hair and black bags under her eyes. She went over the typical English teachers' syllabus, I wasn't really paying attention until she said that she was expecting an essay, due in one week.

The essay would be titled; "a narrative of my childhood", It had to be three pages, double-spaced, Times New Roman font and, twelve-point font. The class let out a sigh and the bell rang before she could assign more 'torture' to us.

"Do you both wanna come over and work on the essay after school?" Wyatt requested.

"Uhhhh, we can meet in the library on Saturday," I replied. Emily merely said; "am out of here, see you later" and off she went. Wyatt looked dejected but said; "sounds good to me,". We all exited the building, and I waited by the curb for Brent. I got in the car and began brainstorming for my essay, as Brent drove me to my next class.

"What're you doing back there?" Brent questioned.

"I have an essay due next week," I replied.

"On the first day?"

"I know, right? It's crazy."

"Please don't tell me you're going to write that paper yourself," Brent asked, as he turned and looked at me through the rearview mirror.

"What do you mean?" I questioned, leaning closer. Brent laughed and continued driving. I pondered over what he'd previously said, until we pulled up to the Technology building.

The Technology building was the most intricately designed building I'd ever seen. It was a cube, all held up on one corner. It seemed to have two support columns on each side. It was all glass, and it seemed like all the levels were slanted.

"The Technology building was designed by students nine years ago," Brent said.

"Cool! Thanks," I replied, as I exited the car. Walking toward the Technology building, I noticed that some freshmen were herding around a Venetian Red Bugatti. Ken exited the passenger side; Keefe exited the driver's side. They both seemed extremely angry, until they noticed that I was approaching them.

Ken's attitude changed, and Keefe ran toward me. He wrapped his arm around my shoulder, and said, "how was your first day of English, Joseph?"

"Cool," I started, "I have an essay due next week."

Ken removed Keefe's arm from around my shoulder and said, "I need to talk to him." Keefe grunted and started walking away.

My attention shifted to Ken, until I heard Keefe say, "just get the bruin to write it for you." I looked back at the laughing Keefe, who looked back at me with a smirk. Keefe could be obnoxious.

I turned to Ken and asked him what class he had. He didn't reply with what I had expected, but instead he said, "you need to keep your head low for some time until tryouts. Also, try and avoid my brother. He only leads to trouble"

Ken continued talking, but I couldn't hear him because I noticed Keefe had gotten on top of a bench and said, "to celebrate the newest addition to SSS, my man, Joseph. We're throwing a party at his place today. If you know where his room is, you're invited."

Ken's was now visibly livid, he said to me, "I'll meet you in the lobby." He gave me a little nudge, inferring that I should begin heading toward the entrance.

I entered the lobby, waited for about four minutes and Ken was coming through the door. Then, I looked through the glass door and saw that a cluster of students had formed around two people fighting. I ran out to see what was happening, it was Ken and Keefe going at it. All the other students were cheering and recording the fight on their phones.

Ken was landing more hits, but due to Keefe's bigger form, he easily wrestled Ken to the ground and placed him in a headlock. I quickly got in between them and separated them. Keefe began laughing as he stood up and fixed his hair. He had a small bruise on his cheek, he said, tauntingly; "let's go again after school."

Ken lunged at him again, but I was able to stop him. To my relief, the late bell rang, and the cluster of students disbanded. I stood there between Ken and Keefe, who were staring each other down. Finally, Keefe gave up, with a little snicker. He got inside his car and roared away. Ken was clear of bruises, but you could tell that he was vigorously upset.

"C'mon, bro," I said to Ken, he began walking toward the building as soon as his brother was out of the parking lot.

Once we entered the empty lobby, the lobbyist glared at us and said, "you're both late, there's no excuse; you had thirty minutes." Ken ignored her and got into the elevator. I followed and apologized to the lady. Ken pressed the "2" button and we began ascending to the second level.

I tried to break the silence by asking him what

class he had, he replied, "the same as you, dipshit."

I took the hint he was pissed, the door then opened and we walked into the class. There was dead silence once we entered the class, everyone was looking at us. The teacher said; "wow, our first scapegoats,". He was a tall, skinny and bald man. He had an almost pale skin and wore suspenders. "You both have detention after school today", he yelled out to us.

Ken walked to one of the two empty seats in the back of the class and sat down without acknowledging the teacher.

"Sorry, sir," I replied. I sat next to Ken, I noticed all the eyes that I'd previously seen outside, staring at us like we were convicts.

"Bring out your laptops and log into your accounts." Everybody pulled one out, except me. I raised my hand and said, "I forgot mine."

The teacher frowned and said, "congrats, you earned yourself another detention tomorrow morning." A few students laughed; I felt stupid. He then continued, "this school comes with a lot of enjoyment and independence, but if you can't follow the rules, you have to pay the consequences." I nodded. not in agreement with him but hoping he'll just stop. He did, he stopped tormenting me and continued yapping about the syllabus.

"What's SSS?" I asked Ken, after he had calmed down.

He looked at me and veered off to look at his laptop. After about three minutes, he said, "Sky Suite Squad. It's supposed to be a club of up to twenty-nine Pinnacle members, but there are only about fifteen because Keefe is the president, and Glenn vice president. Plus, they only accept people that they like."

"Are you in it?" I whispered back.

"Sadly. Next year, I'm gonna have to run it. It's a school-recognized club."

"Did your brother come up with the idea?" I questioned.

"No, he's not smart enough to brainstorm something like that. It was some guy named Brad, like three decades ago, or something like that. They worship him like he's the father of all Sky Suite Squad members."

I was going to ask another question, until Mr. Callahan, the teacher, said, "you boys don't want another detention, neither do you want me to separate you, do you?" We both shook our heads and he said, "then get back to work." I put my head down and fell asleep, until I was woken up by the bell.

Ken and I served our after-school detention, writing "I will not be late to class", one hundred times on the board.

On my way out of the building, my phone rang. The screen didn't show a name, but I could tell it was my mom's number.

"Hey, Mom."

"Joey! We've missed you! How's your first day going?" she asked.

"Eh, good. Classes are a bit longer, but the teachers are cool." I intentionally didn't tell her about the two detentions I had received because she would have freaked out and called the administration. I heard Ken call my name somewhere behind me, "mom, I have to go, I'll call you back in later," I said to her, forgetting to ask her how she could afford AA's tuition.

"I'll give you a ride," said Ken, then added, "I already told Brent".

"Oh thanks. Are we going somewhere or something?" I questioned, out of curiosity.

"I mean, I was gonna take you back to the suite, but if you wanna grab something to eat, that's fine too," Ken replied.

"Yeah, that sounds good." Moments later, Ken's personal car pulled up, by the curb. There wasn't anyone in the driver's seat, so I was a bit confused. These were the things that I would have to get used to if I didn't want to constantly look weird at this school.

Once we were seated in the car, we reclined our seats and began to watch Love and Living Animals, the stupidest show ever, but it was still funny.

In the episode we watched, the big-cat zookeeper was cheated on by his wife, so he trained a lion to attack people, when he found a way to take the lion home, he'd forgotten it was his birthday.

A surprise party had been organized by his wife, oblivious of this, he brought the Lion home. As he opened the door and his family and friends shouted; "surprise!", the Lion got agitated and began to attack all the party guests.

By the time the dust settled, the Lion had mauled everyone at the party, including the zookeeper's wife. The Lion was returned to the zoo while the zookeeper was arrested and tried in court. He was found guilty and sentenced to living with the Lion, in a cage for the rest of his life.

I still don't understand how the actors could read the absurd plot and still be willing to act it out, it got me scratching my head for answers, so I didn't care too much about how absurd it was, it was engaging.

We finally arrived at our destination, Ken's car stopped, the doors flung open and we got out of the car. We walked into a massive, high wall, circular building.

It had many restaurants, from everyday fast-food places, to AA exclusive fine-dining options. There were exotic corners, which was ironic, because the entire place was shaped like a huge circle. The corners had food from different countries; Chinese food, Indian food and various Middle Eastern restaurants.

"We call this place Lockwood," Ken said with a chuckle. That was the name of the lunchroom on

Love and Living Animals, where the most drama happened. "All the fast food restaurants are free, because they come with the tuition. You just order, scan your ID, and those large tubes drop your food onto your table, in about four minutes. It's incredible! They use a microchip inside your ID. AA's architecture and engineering is insane," Ken explained.

I picked up a map idling away on a nearby seat. Glancing through it, I noticed the simple and efficient food delivery system at Lockwood, it was impressive. Lockwood was located right in the center of the campus; this provided all students, easy access to it. "How isn't everybody here obese?" I asked.

"P.E. is insane," he replied.

"Well, uh, where do you like to eat?" I questioned. He gladly pointed at a restaurant, about eighty feet away. It was named Pancraziano's.

"All I really eat is their pizza. It's freakin' amazing, dude," he said, and he began smiling, just thinking about it.

"Well, we can split one," I said. He just looked at me like I was crazy.

He replied with one word, before he began walking toward Pancraziano's. "No."

Once we arrived at the restaurant, he walked up to one of the twelve digital screens. None of the restaurants had workers, which I found crazy.

He customized his large pizza, with just the classic

pineapple and ham. When it was my turn, I selected medium but before I could place the order, Ken stepped between me and the touch screen, "what are you doing? Get large, bro. If you can't finish it, just toss it in the fridge.

You have P.E. first thing tomorrow, and you're gonna need all the energy you can get.

I thought about it and concluded he must be right. I ordered the same thing he did.

They had a glass wall next to the last register, through which anyone could watch the pizza being made by the robotic arms that looked like they were made to build cars.

Ken and I strolled toward a black wall that looked like it was somewhere that a restaurant used to be.

There was a magenta colored door with a single, golden pull bar. On top was the inscription; "SSS". I assumed it stood for the club that I'd been recently inducted into.

We were about to go inside, but then Ken had some type of epiphany and turned to one of the regular tables. We sat down across from each other, Ken pressed a button on the side of the table, the sides of the table rose up and water flooded onto it. The water bubbled a little bit then drained away magically. "It's disinfectant juice," Ken explained before I even asked.

Suddenly, two metal rods lowered our pizzas in

front of us. We opened the boxes that read the name of the restaurant, and the aroma of the pizza flooded my nostrils. I felt my body quiver, starting from my mouth. I took the first bite, it melted in my mouth immediately, releasing a myriad of flavors.

The sauce formed a layer over my tongue that magnified the taste of the cheese and all the toppings. I sighed with every bite and before I knew it, there was no pizza left. "Are we gonna get another?" I pleaded.

Ken shook his head and explained, "the algorithm basically just allows you to eat enough to survive. It calculates calories and every day you need to have exactly enough calories required to stay healthy.

If you skip a meal, it automatically sends your most ordered food to your room, which is especially convenient during midterms and finals." I understood what he said, but I still couldn't stop thinking about what P.E. class was going to be like the next day.

When Ken and I got back to our building, I ran into Wyatt. He was waiting for me on the lobby couch. Once he saw me, he walked toward me briskly and asked, "where have you been?"

Ken glanced over as Wyatt walked toward the elevator. "I went to Lockwood with Ken," I replied.

"Oh darn, I wanted to grab lunch with you. Have you met my roommate?"

“Sorry, you should’ve let me know beforehand,” I replied. When I tried to walk away, he began talking to me again.

“I’ve told Clyde so much about you. He’s probably so eager to meet you,” Wyatt said.

“Oh, that’s cool, maybe we can grab lunch sometime.” I replied then tried to walk away again.

Wyatt stepped in front of me and cried out, “let’s go for dinner tonight!” I didn’t want to tell him about the party because he would try and come. It wasn’t that I was embarrassed to have a friend like him, but I knew he’d just be the laughingstock the entire time.

I hesitated and in the midst of coming up with an excuse, I instinctively said, “sounds good.”

He smiled cheerily and said, "meet me here at seven." He walked away without another word and awkwardly smiled at me from the elevator. He made me feel uncomfortable, but I was preoccupied trying to plan my night out.

5

Pancrazies & Clyde

I got into the elevator, and on the way up, I began thinking; If we got there for seven fifteen and ate by seven-twenty, I could get out before eight and arrive back for the party at ten. Shortly after completing my thought, I arrived in my room, and my phone began ringing again. I'd obviously forgotten to call my mom back.

Ken was just sitting on the couch and on the phone with some girl. I went upstairs to my room. I gave my mom a rundown of my day—of course, leaving out the detention part, I asked about conferences, she told me they were in two months, I sighed with relief.

I was able to speak with my sister; Elizabeth, but when it was time for me to talk to my stepdad, I lied about my phone almost dying. Talking with my mom and my sister and not with my stepdad brought back memories of my dad. Only if he had not died, I would talk with him, every day.

Flashes of my 4th grade came back, how my dad died, killing another person, as a drunk driver. My mom told me their marriage was very rough during that time, and he became an alcoholic.

The other family decided to sue us, that's how my mom met Brad. He was our lawyer, he helped us dodge the case somehow. I could not trust Brad, something about him seemed way too shady.

Ever since he married my mom, he's wanted my sister and I out of the picture. We hardly talked about my dad with Brad around, he just had to be in control of everything. He was not much of a dad to us because we did not really like him.

My sister and I had a very good relationship with our dad, he was fun to be with, he loved us both so much.

That phone call got me thinking about my dad and how much I miss him, if I still miss my dad so much, how would Elizabeth feel, I thought.

I had two hours before I had to meet Wyatt, so I decided to pack my bag and take a nap.

I woke up at eight thirty, threw on new clothes,

and sprinted by a sleeping Ken, to get to the elevator. Once I arrived in the lobby, I ran up to Wyatt and apologized. "It's fine, man. I just got down here five minutes ago. I was drained from classes today."

We both laughed at our tardiness and proceeded to go outside. Only then did I realize that I had no way of contacting Brent, I would have to take the bus or another form of transportation.

Wyatt, interrupted my thought, saying "Clyde's at the inner AA shopping plaza, so he said he'll meet us at Lockwood".

I nodded then asked, "what are we waiting for? The bus won't come for another fifteen minutes." I didn't feel like waiting, so I walked up to Chris at the lobby and asked for Brent's phone number. In about five minutes, Brent arrived and had a withdrawn look, once he saw Wyatt with me.

He glared at me and I ignored him. Once in the car, we started watching our favorite show again. I had to watch episode six again with Wyatt because he had not watched it, the last he watched was episode 5.

When we arrived at Lockwood, Wyatt and I got out of the car and saw a figure that seemed to be waiting for us. I assumed it was Clyde, we walked over to meet him. He resembled a young Robert Downey Jr.

He appeared somewhat emotionless, had spiky-looking hair and very sharp facial features. He looked a bit older than fifteen or sixteen, I noticed the stripes on his collar, which resembled the sophomore class.

"Hey, you must be Clyde," I said to him. He smiled and shook my hand. He had bags under his eyes, but once we got into the main Lockwood cafeteria, they disappeared.

His teeth sparkled as he smiled at the smell of food. Lockwood wasn't too crowded; I noticed a lot of students eating while using their phones or laptops.

Wyatt leaned towards me and said, "am glad you met Clyde Bushburg. He draws the comics for the Almington Almanack, the school newspaper. Everybody knows him, and he's so good at drawing that they considered upgrading him to a golden status.

Every sensible bruin would accept, but not him. Instead, he drew a piece about how the administrative system at AA is corrupt, so they downgraded him from silver to bronze. That's how he became my roommate. Oh, and he loves to eat. Instead of giving him credits, they give him complimentary meals as a reward for his skills."

I could only reply with a simple, "Wow."

By the time Wyatt finished his prologue, he'd already found something else to say. "Oh, and if you haven't noticed yet, Almington basically has celebrities."

Clyde turned to us and said, "I'm gonna go grab

some Indian food." Before we could even answer, he'd disappeared to the Indian Spice corner.

"Have you ever tried Pancraziano's?" I asked.

"What type of question is that? Everybody here goes pancrazy for Pancraziano's! See what I did there?" he yelled. The crazy line at Pancraziano's confirmed the claim he'd made.

While we were in line, I asked, "so who are the celebrities you were talking about? That seems a bit weird, considering we're fourteen to eighteen."

"Age is just a number," he replied with a smile. Then he continued, "well, it's just about the descendants of the founders of the school. They all have unique and strange last names, and all have two kids, which I find too coincidental to be true".

Not done talking, Wyatt continued; "there's the Hollowvales, Ken and Keefe; the Violetcliffs, Emily and Emelia; the Summerforts, Glenn and Gloria, Danielle and David Merribridge; and Cheyenne and Charlie Van Perrel.

I swear they have access to some drug that makes them good at sports, 'cause they're all good at sports. Those are the exclusives of the exclusive. They all drive expensive cars and live the most lavish lifestyles".

At this point, all I could do was stand in line with my garrulous friend and look at other students munching away.

We arrived at the front of the line; we both ordered the same thing I'd ordered earlier. It happened to be Wyatt's favorite too. Wyatt called Clyde and we met up and found a table to sit. Clyde's food had an aroma that was insane. It smelled so good and looked perfect. I said a prayer and began biting into the deliciousness.

"So, you draw?" I asked Clyde. He placed another bite of food in his mouth, so he didn't have to verbally reply. Instead he nodded. We were all enjoying our food so much, it was like we were on a different planet. We were in silence and about three slices in, I noticed two figures plop down in front of us, their pizzas arriving shortly after. Emily was on one side and Ken on the other. Clyde was completely unfazed, he continued smacking his lips.

Wyatt, however, got nervy, I looked at them in confusion. "Wassup, guys. What brings you here?" I was more confused by Ken because the party was supposed to be in another hour.

"I noticed you when I was ordering, so I called Ken to ask if the party was off or something, he told me he just saw you run out, he agreed to convince Keefe to call off the party; we met here," Emily explained.

"Wow. Nice," I replied.

"I see you've met Clyde." Ken said to me, while glaring at Clyde. They exchanged hateful looks, but I was able to break the silence by introducing them both to Wyatt. Ken seemed really relaxed and kind of happy to meet Wyatt. He was like a whole different person after his nap.

We continued to eat and joke around, we were able to convince Clyde to draw a picture of us all, on Wyatt's pizza box. I felt in my element because Ken and Wyatt were both making us all laugh.

There was a point that Clyde fell on the floor laughing. Emily had a good sense of humor too, she related well with all the guys. Before we noticed it, we'd been sitting there laughing for almost three hours. We were the only ones left in the entire Lockwood complex and were just enjoying ourselves. I couldn't remember being that happy since Disney with my dad when I was eight.

Later, a grumpy old man walked up to us and said, "we're about to flush the floors, so I'm going to need you guys to leave."

"Oh! You guys need to see this!" Emily said.

"What?" I questioned as we finally got up. Our trash was sucked up through the trash tubes. "Every night at twelve, these huge magnets suck up the chairs and tables, then the floor gets covered in disinfectant juice." Clyde explained. He and Emily were the only ones who had seen it before.

After we exited, we got up against the glass doors and watched every table and chair get sucked up into midair, while the clear, bubbly juice covered the entire plaza floor. After about ten minutes, it drained, the chairs and tables were then lowered to the floor.

"My sister's gonna be here soon," Emily said. She said bye to each of us and suggested the creation of a group chat, with all of us in it. Ken hesitated, realizing he'd be friends with a bruin but eventually accepted. She created it and named it "Pancrazies & Clyde". It was an inside joke we had.

Ken suggested giving everyone else a ride since we were all going to the Merribridge.

We continued to laugh and joke around in the car while watching Love and Living Animals, which Clyde had surprisingly never heard of or seen.

I realized that if this was going to be a group of my friends, this year would be the best school year I'd ever have.

6

P.E. Chamber

The next morning, I arrived at the P.E. chamber, twenty-minutes early. The building was gigantic, it had an extremely high ceiling, the walls had enlarged portraits and paintings of AA sports individual achievers and teams; through the ages.

From what I could tell, it must be a great honor to have your photo or painting on P.E. chamber walls. Perhaps, my picture will hang up there, one day, I thought.

The sound of the arriving elevator snapped me out of my daydreaming.

Having some time to spare before class began, I walked around the facility, it had;

- Indoor track fields
- Indoor lacrosse, soccer and football fields
- An aquatic center with two warm water Swimming pools
- Two Olympic size swimming pools
- Walking track and stretching areas
- Whirlpools and Saunas
- Basketball/Volleyball/Wallyball/Pickleball courts
- Indoor tennis courts
- A mini clinic
- A smoothie & snack cafe
- Health & fitness counseling office
- Massage studios
- Three fully equipped Gymnasiums
- Gaming studios

There were more amenities within the P.E. Chamber, but I did not have enough time to see all, I had to go to class at “Gym A”.

“Gym A”, had two doors on opposite walls. One read "Boys" and the other read "Girls." There were three instructors standing in the center of the gym with a clipboard.

There were about sixty students in the class, and once we had all gotten into the class, I heard the thundering boom of a man's voice. "Good morning! I'm Mr. Struck. I am accompanied by my two co-instructors: Mrs. Spicer and Ms. Fastovsky." He gestured to them and they waved accordingly.

Mr. Struck was a very short man, he must have been a wrestler, at some point in his life, I thought. He was stocky, looked fit and strong. With a shape like that, it was difficult to guess his age.

He wore high-waisted shorts that came to above his knees, and socks that almost reached his knees. He wore white tennis shoes and a gray shirt that read "ARMY" in black letters.

He had a mustache that made him appear goofy. He would be a rough and tough instructor, I concluded in my mind.

Mrs. Spicer had a delicately slim figure, she had brown hair and brown eyes. She must be in her mid-thirties, probably an overall nice instructor, I imagined.

Ms. Fastovsky appeared caffeine-deprived and tired. She must be in her forties but looked like a sixty-something. She appeared detached and exhausted.

Mr. Struck shouted; "if I call your name, go to "wall 1". Once I'm through with my class, Mrs. Spicer will call names, and whoever she calls should proceed to "wall 2". Lastly, Ms. Fastovsky will go, I think you all know how this goes." He was obviously expecting a response that he didn't get.

He began calling names, and I paid no attention until he called Glenn's name. I looked up and watched him walk toward his wall. I began to scan the class for any other student I could've known, it was only then that I stumbled upon Keefe, who was asleep against the wall.

Mrs. Spicer began calling names and when she called Keefe, he remained completely oblivious.

She called his name about three times, staring right at him, then Mr. Struck trotted up to his ear and screamed at the top of his lungs, "Keefe Hollowvale!" Keefe resurrected in a split second, laughter echoed throughout "Gym A"; Keefe proceeded to his wall and Mrs. Spicer finished her roll call.

Everyone else, whose names were not called belonged to Ms. Fastovsky's class, so we all proceeded to "wall 3".

Mr. Struck looked around to make sure that everything was in order before he instructed us. "These are going to be your classes for the rest of the year.

Boys, please proceed to the boys' locker room, and girls to the girls." We all complied and proceeded to line up outside of our locker room doors. Mr. Struck came by and unlocked the door for us, letting us into the biggest locker room I've ever seen.

There were small changing rooms numbered one

to thirty. There was an individual bathtub with a showerhead, bench, mirror, and a locker on the wall. There was a lounge chair, personal water bottle-filling station, water fountain, sink, soap dispenser, tissue dispenser, a toilet and an intercom on the ceiling. It was nothing like my middle-school locker room.

Mr. Struck then began his tour of the extremely oversized locker room. "This is the laundry room," he said, leading us to a room with thirty washers and thirty dryers. "We ask that you wash your gym clothes separately from your regular clothes because you will all be sweating; a lot," Mr. Struck added, as he left the room.

We followed him down a hall to a metal door. He unlocked it and opened the door with a creak. The room was cloudy and had a huge metal chest against the center wall. "This is the ice room. Ice baths are popular here, and I would, a hundred percent recommend it, at the end of every class.

"If you want to get ice, you unlock the door, one at a time, open this chest, and scoop ice into your ice tubs. This room is very cold, so please always keep the door shut.

Now, on a more serious note; there are three things I don't permit in this locker room—hazing, horseplay, and trapping people in this room.

Now, if you do get trapped in the ice room, press the emergency release button; this red button here, the door will shoot open at an incredible speed, tossing back anyone trying to pin the door shut.

This will also ring the intercom alarm, and I will be immediately notified of the incident. I'm not going to state the consequences of bad behavior. I'll just leave them for you to find out yourselves."

Mr. Struck continued down the hall to an open lounge, with five TVs, a series of lounge chairs, a ping-pong table, and some other features you'd find in a typical lounge.

Now, you must be outside at your walls, ready to go at nine fifteen every day you have this class. The doors are open from 7 a.m. to 7 p.m., so if you're lame enough to spend your time in the locker room, go ahead. Don't forget to bring athletic shoes. If you forget, you can borrow some for the day, but I can't guarantee pristine condition training shoes."

Mr. Struck walked over to his desk, picked up his clipboard, led us back to the lounge and yelled; "everybody, have a seat. I'm going to call names. When I call your name, walk out into this hall and take a left to my office. I will hand you a piece of paper.

It will have your name on it, your room number, and your four-digit door PIN, required to get into your room. I want you all to go to your locker rooms, change into your uniforms, and go straight to your walls."

We waited for the first name to be called. Keefe finally noticed me and walked over with Glenn. They sat next to me and said, "what're you doing in this class?"

"I have no clue what you're talking about," I replied.

"This is a senior class, bro. Talk to Mr. Struck, I think your schedule might be messed up," Glenn stated. That was the first time they were being serious. It was probably because they did not drink much the previous night. The entire class waited in silence; it was way too early to cause commotion. After about ten names, I was called, and I walked into Mr. Struck's office.

"Joseph?" he asked.

"Uh, yeah, that's me," I replied. He handed me a card that read, "Room 12: PIN - 2917." He wrote my name down on his clipboard and I asked, "I heard this is a senior-level class and I'm a sophomore. Is there a mistake?"

He looked up at me and said, "I received a special request from Coach Morris to place you in this class. Can you please leave my office now?" I turned around and took a long walk to my room. I put on the maroon shorts with embroidered AA and the plain gray shirt that had two black stripes. I walked out and waited against "wall 3".

About eight minutes later, all the girls emerged at once, wearing the same type of uniform as the boys, but everyone had the complete four-striped shirt, while I had two.

Mr. Struck got in the middle of the gym and said, "today we will be completing our fitness test. There are three stations that will be rotated through: sit-ups, push-ups, and the 2-mile run. You'll rotate with your instructor, as you know, today will be the easiest day of the year."

"Now, I'm going to read out the ranges so listen carefully. For push-ups, boys must get a minimum of forty-five, and girls thirty. If you can't reach it, you'll be stuck at your station for the duration of the class, until you do.

It's best you get it the first time. The Target Healthy Number, or "THN" is going to be low this year, at forty-five for boys and thirty for girls.

For sit-ups, we decided to make an exception this year and reduce the minimum to sixty for boys and fifty for girls. The "THN" is going to be sixty for boys and fifty for girls."

"Lastly, the 2-mile run. The "THN" for the boys is ten minutes – fifty seconds while the girls have twelve minutes – twenty-five seconds. Ms. Fastovsky 's class will start at sit-ups; Ms. Spicer's class; with the push-ups; my class follow me; we're going out to the track, we are not using the indoor tracks today, you all should sweat a little."

Once Mr. Struck's class left, Ms. Fastovsky yelled, "everybody, go to the double doors", we opened the huge storage closet, and laid the mats, to start sit-ups. Ms. Fastovsky instructed us to partner up, I chose the kid sitting right next to me. His name was Ethan, he was also in my English class.

We had a little small talk before we began the sit-ups. I was able to get sixty done to hit the "THN", so did Ethan. We rotated to push-ups, Ethan and I, did the forty-five push-ups needed for "THN".

We then stood by the door waiting to proceed to the 2-mile run.

"So, what class do you have next? Ethan asked.

"Government," I replied, "What about you?" I questioned.

"Math," he replied. Then he continued, "I heard that government is really hard."

I just nodded because the conversation was getting a bit sluggish. Ethan picks his words, and that bores me.

About fifteen minutes later, Mrs. Spicer's class walked back into the room, each of them looking exhausted. We rotated outside and walked to the starting line.

Ms. Fastovsky began giving instructions. "As most of you should know by now, it's a 2-mile race, for a "THN" of ten minutes – fifty seconds for the boys and twelve minutes – twenty-five seconds for the girls.

The fully automatic digital timing system will display your time, watch the board, it should guide your speed and pacing."

She shouted; "three, two, one—go!" Everybody shot off from the starting line, I seemed to be at the back. I knew if I increased my pace, I'd burn out by the end, so I maintained my position in last place.

By the second lap, many of the girls and a few of the boys had begun slowing down. I started catching up with the rest of the pack by the last lap. At this point, a lot of runners were beginning to fade out, but I had to push through to get ahead.

I began sprinting through the last two hundred meters, I passed everyone but two boys and the girl who had been in the lead the entire time.

All four of us led the group and finished within split seconds of each other, hitting the "THN", quite easily.

We walked back into "Gym A" to join all the other students to pack up. That did not take too long. With everything properly arranged, class was dismissed and as I joined the other boys to line up to go into the boys' locker room, I felt someone pull me by shirt collar.

"How'd you do?" Glenn asked.

"Nine minutes, fifty-six seconds," I replied, without turning to look at him. I wasn't the biggest fan of Glenn and Keefe's because they were a bit too stuck-up for me. They always felt a sense of self-importance, that they were higher than everybody in the school, including the teachers.

"Nice, but you'll have to do better if you plan on making the lacrosse team," Glenn added.

"Oh, please!" I heard Keefe shout, as he walked up to us. "He's already on the team. This kid single-handedly took his freshmen lacrosse team to the state champs, bro," he added.

My dad was a professional lacrosse player, and he always wanted me to follow in his footsteps, even though it never provided enough salary for him.

He won the state championships in Nebraska all four years of his high school and all four years of his college. If I had to say so myself, I was an exceptional lacrosse player, and I felt I had a lot of potential to go division one.

"Is that true, Joseph?" Glenn asked with a smirk.

"Well, it wasn't done single-handedly," I stated, until I was interrupted by the hollering of the two obnoxious boys.

We got into the locker room, Mr. Struck said, "you have about an hour of free time until the bell rings. Spend it wisely." I went to my room and took a cold shower. Shortly after, I heard a loud knock on my door. I was only in a towel, so it wasn't my initial response to open the door, until I thought it could be Mr. Struck. I opened the door, Glenn and Keefe came running into my room. Keefe sat down in the lounge chair and Glenn sat on a bench.

"What's up? I asked them.

"Nothing, bro. We just came to chill. Do you wanna party tonight?" Keefe asked me.

"No, sorry, I have an English paper due," I replied. I considered myself an introverted extrovert. I didn't really like parties and public places, but I liked hanging out with those close to me, and when I was around them, I talked way more than I did with others.

"C'mon, man, you've gotta get adapted to the SSS lifestyle!" Keefe added. "I can get a bruin to do your work for you, for a cool hundred, if you want. All on me," Glenn said.

"No thanks, I'm working on it with some friends from my English class, and I told them I'd come." There was an odd silence, as Glenn and Keefe exchanged a similar look.

Keefe glared at me and asked, "does one of those friends happen to be Wyatt Heffler?" I nodded, and they both left my room without a word. I had a feeling that I'd somehow let them down, but at the same time, I didn't care too much.

7

The jigsaw grinder

The bell rang. I hurried out to my ride, to avoid contact with Keefe and Glenn. The social studies building was a magnificent and elegant building. It housed the geography, history and government classes. I'd heard a lot of cool stories about the geography class. I heard that the basement was a virtual-reality chamber, that could take anyone, anywhere around the world, and that it was updated every year, through satellite imaging.

I walked into the building and took the elevator to the eighth level, where my class was. My teacher's name was written on the board. It read, Mr. H. I presumed he had a very long last name. I was the fourth kid to get to the classroom, a few minutes later, more students came rushing in. I noticed that Clyde and Emily were both in this class.

They were talking to each other; Clyde was holding a journal in his hand and had a drawing pencil on his ear. Emily was wearing a burgundy sweater. Clyde had his scarf; he was wearing round glasses for some reason. They caught a glimpse of me, and their faces lit up. They sat on either side of me and we began talking. "So how was your first day of P.E.?" Clyde asked.

"It was easy, but I heard the first day is always easy," I replied. They nodded in agreement and I asked, "where are you guys coming from?"

Emily answered and said, "Art 3 G/T."

"Wow, that must be hard," I replied, but before they could answer, a familiar face stumbled into the room.

"Hello, everyone!" said Chris. He walked up to the board and finished writing his name. "Mr. Heverley" it read. He looked around the class and said, "well, I'm happy to see some familiar faces around here." I could feel him staring straight at me, but I chose not to look back at him, instead, I pretended to scratch something off my desk.

My suspicion was confirmed by the looks that Clyde and Emily gave me through awkward silence. I looked up at him, and he nodded at me. I looked to the side and saw Clyde, already drawing a comic or something in his journal.

"Well, I will tell you guys a bit about me, we'll get started on some icebreakers." Chris said and walked over to his desk, picking up his presentation remote clicker. "Well, my name is Chris Heverley. I graduated from this school six years ago, I attended and graduated from Loyola College with a degree in Government and Environmental Studies. My love for AA brought me back to teach American Government class. I'm the head coach of the varsity swimming team and am a dorm custodian". He laughed a little, but nobody else did. "Tough crowd," he mumbled, then continued. "Well, on that note, let's get started on some icebreakers!"

He walked around and passed out a sheet of paper, with about thirty boxes and something printed at the top that read, "Nobody can sign more than once" It had random statements, such as, "Been to Germany," with a line underneath, so the student could sign it. The point of the game was to get us to talk to as many students as possible to fill up all the boxes.

It was a good idea, but I expected Chris, of all people, to understand that these activities never work, they only achieve the goal of making students hate their teachers more for forcing them to talk to random students, in an already awkward situation.

I walked up to some kid sitting in front of the class and asked, "hey, have you or a relative been to an AA football game?" "Nah, man, do you have a relative that's been to AA?" he replied. I shook my head and we parted ways. Chris stood at the front of the class, smiling at us running around like chickens.

After about twenty minutes of no progress, we all started lying about what we had and hadn't done. We sat in our seats once everyone was finished. "If you didn't know already, you can just call me Chris. I'm probably your coolest teacher." That statement already had loads of flaws in it, speaking in monotone did not help him at all.

We could all see that he so badly wanted to relate with us. Was he reliving his AA student days, did he miss out on something while at AA, I thought.

He went over the syllabus, toward the end of class, he said, "well, it was great getting to know you guys, but the teacher trend," he stated with a giggle, "are diagnostic papers. Teachers will be grading pretty leniently; we just want to see what you already know.". The class sighed and grunted.

Then some kid in the back shouted out, "It's the first day, c'mon man!" Chris's vibrant expression, slowly faded

"Well, I want you guys to pick a branch of government and write a three-page essay on it. I want it in the Modern Language Association - (MLA) format, with citations.

You have about fifteen minutes to start brainstorming before the bell rings," Chris finished and retreated to his desk.

He seemed a bit sad, but something on his laptop seemed to rejuvenate him quickly. Emily, Clyde, and I aligned our desks in a conference format and began to quickly exchange ideas.

Clyde handed us each a piece of paper, I began with, "what branch are we doing?"

"What do you think the easiest is?" Emily asked.

"I think the executive, 'cause it's really just the president," I said. Then Clyde rotated his paper toward us. I thought he'd been drawing comics or something, but he'd created a detailed outline and flow chart on the judicial branch.

"See, I agree with executive branch, but you can't possibly come up with three whole pages on it. However, the judicial branch is different," he said, as he flipped the page over, revealing more writing.

"How'd you know?" Emily asked.

"Chris and I spoke about it briefly this morning, when I found out he was my teacher," Clyde replied. I never thought that Clyde was much of a smart-type guy, but he clearly was. Emily and I began copying down general ideas, periodically looking over our shoulders, making sure Chris didn't catch us.

We didn't really have to worry about that because he seemed consumed by something on his laptop. The bell rang halfway into our copying Clyde's outline. Clyde stood up, snapped a picture of his paper, and sent it to us in the group chat.

As we left the class, we all talked about the night before, when we all received a confused reply from Ken. We laughed about it and parted ways.

When I arrived at my Mathematics building, I noticed the details on the building. There were small math symbols all over the tall, green edifice. It looked about fifteen stories tall, and all the windows had a green tint. In front of the building was the statue of a man I didn't recognize. But when I got closer, I noticed the small etchings of math symbols, then I saw his name; Srinivasa Ramanujan; interesting, I thought and walked away.

I remembered Wyatt was in my class, so I waited in the lobby for him. "Joey, over here!" I heard him yell to me. I walked over to him; we took the elevator to the fifteenth floor. Wyatt was seated to my left, another student with the same name as I, sat on my right.

"Hello class," I heard the teacher say. I'd thought the teacher was a student waiting for someone. She was short and skinny, it might be better to describe as being frail looking, her short black hair amplified her petit size.

Once we were all seated, she wrote her name on the board. It read Mrs. Banaszewski. She then began telling us about herself. "Hello class, my name is Mrs. Sarah Banaszewski. The 'Z' in Banaszewski is silent, but if it's easier for you guys to call me Mrs.

B, be my guest.

I was born in Spain and moved to the U.S, when I was fourteen. Here, I met the Polish man, I now call my husband. I've spent a lot of my adult life in the hospital.

I got a pacemaker inserted at twenty-nine and have battled with two types of cancer since"; she paused, then continued, "the reason I tell you this, is to encourage you, follow your passion, chase your dreams, let nothing hinder from achieving your goals, don't stop, don't give up, keep pushing, keep striving to be the best version of you. Your best you is around the corner, waiting to be discovered – go for it".

The class erupted with cheers and clapped till she signaled for us to stop. Through my peripheral vision, I could see a tall, slim girl, about four seats away, wiping her eyes.

When the class was calm, Mrs. B walked over to her laptop and turned on the presentation.

"I understand that a lot of you have other classes that are equally demanding, you'll need to prioritize, you'll need to put a lot of effort into this class, possibly even more," said Ms. B.

Going further, she said; "the Algebra Exam - AE is mainly Algebra 2. The AE is a test that you must take at the end of every school year. The test is two hundred fifty questions, you have to get at least an 800/1000 by senior year, or you will have to take a 'specialized year,' which is no fun – trust me."

I was confused by her last statement, but she continued; "they claim that if you have to take a fifth year, you'll never graduate, because the fifth-year test they give you is harder than the actual test, and the stress levels are through the roof", she concluded.

After she explained the syllabus, she gave us a diagnostic Algebra 1 test, to see how much we remember and if she had to do a review or not.

When class was over, I gave Wyatt a ride to the Merribridge. I invited him up to my room, where we played video games until very late. That was a great way to spend Friday night.

The next day, I met with Wyatt at 9:00 a.m., we had a cool day planned. "Ready?" I asked him. He nodded, Brent drove us to the library, which was called Grand Perriman Parlor. When we arrived, I stood before the enormous building that looked like a Rubik's cube, same shape, same colors. A vibrant and interesting place to study, I thought.

We walked in and I saw the floor layout. There were eight stories, the first three were mainly for books, with some study rooms here and there. The next two levels had computers, but they were rarely used because they were monitored, most students had personal laptops. The top three levels were all study pods.

We made our way to the highest level, which had more people than I expected, being a Saturday morning. Ken and Emily were unable to join us because there was a huge party the night before, so they'd decided to sleep in.

Ken had tried to pressure me to go, but I chose not to because I had too much schoolwork that I wanted to get done, over the weekend.

Wyatt and I spent four hours writing the essay about our individual childhoods and on the role of the judiciary in government. We felt we did a great job too. Around 2:00pm, we called Clyde, Emily and Ken, we met with them at Lockwood, grabbed some carry out pizza, drove back to Merribridge, went up to our Sky Suite to binge on the dumbest show in television history; Love and Living Animals.

At about 5:45pm, Ken suggested we put ourselves out of the misery that Love and Living Animals show had become, it had begun to drag as they stretched the episodes. Episode 28 was downright boring.

"The football game is at 7:00pm, we need to go now guys," Ken announced. We packed up, got down to the car garage and Ken drove us to the football game.

When we arrived, we noticed the energy right away. AA was a big school with a lot of students, so they had to accommodate with huge bleachers, which were filled.

We had a suite, so we were sheltered from the drizzle. The players came out of the tunnel, in their white-and-maroon jerseys. The suite was all glass so we could see through on all sides. Other suites had mostly adults and other people who seemed like scouts.

They were writing on clipboards most of the game. In a split second, I caught the glimpse of a familiar face among the scouts. Mr. Struck was giving them small bios on the players who they were interested in, then I leaned over to Ken and asked, "what is Struck doing here?"

"Mr. Struck is the athletics coordinator here, he's pretty in touch with all the players and coaches," Ken replied.

I was intrigued by the strange experience of the live game in a suite surrounded by all that I had never experienced.

The noise was incredibly loud, especially when they scored a touchdown. I couldn't imagine what it would be like to be in the stands, amid all the noise. Soon after, the game concluded, with Almington Academy winning 46 - 3 over Westbrook Academy, last year's regional champion.

On Sunday, I went to the chapel with Clyde, the only other practicing Christian among the students I relate with. After Church, I met with my counselor. His name was Mr. Theft, but he went by Brian, he must be in his late fifties but looked a lot younger.

He was a tall African American former basketball player, who'd been known for his incredible AA illogical theories. His most popular illogical theory was that the AA administration was run by robots, because nobody ever saw them.

Another was that all the people who had figured out the 'grave secrets' of AA, were offered jobs at AA, in exchange for their silence. That one rang throughout the campus out of irony, due to the fact he was now a guidance counselor at AA, and he probably knows the 'grave secrets' of AA. No one took him seriously, some thought that he was delusional or merely craving attention.

"Joseph?" he asked.

"Yup," I replied.

"Yeah, so I just wanted to call you in here to discuss your course plan. Especially because you were not at AA for your freshman year. Luckily, we were able to transfer all your credits from your old school, so you don't have to take many freshmen classes, I was informed that you wanted to go into zoology?"

"Uh, yes I do, but I'm not looking too far into the future right now."

"Well, you might want to change that pretty soon, son. Also, I've been told that the zoology teachers steal animals from the Central State Zoo for dissections at anatomy classes," he said, leaning in toward me.

"Are all your assertions a joke, or are you serious?", I demanded, not in the mood for jokes on a Sunday morning.

"I'm a counselor, right?" he replied, with a wink. I

felt irritated but had to hide it. Then he continued, "go to the administrative building and ask to speak with an administrator. I swear it's the algorithm, son. They're all robots, and don't want their secret getting out." I chuckled, until I realized that he was being completely serious.

"Well, is there anything else?" I asked, gesturing to the papers on his desk.

"Yeah, uh, since you missed your freshman year AE, you'll need to fill out an exempt form and hope that those robots accept it. If not, you'll have to take it this year, going off your prior knowledge," he concluded, handing me a yellow form that read, ACADEMY EXAM 1 - EXEMPT FORM. I began filling it out, at his office table but he shooed me out of his room so that he could tend to other students.

8

Navigating the maze

A month of regular school later, in zoology class, we had our first field trip. We were going to the only reasonable place of interest to me; the Central State Zoo. We were supposed to get into groups of six, so Wyatt and I partnered up and grouped with four other boys.

Their names were Trevor, Travis, Alex, and Devin. Trevor and Travis were twins but had polar-opposite personalities. Trevor was a bookworm who had an extensive knowledge of animals and they live. Travis was completely oblivious nine times out of ten.

Alex and Devin were pretty laid back, but they never seemed like they wanted to be on the field trip.

We got to the entrance of the zoo; Mr. Scott handed each group a paper. We designated Trevor to be the writer, mainly because he'd be the one coming up with all the answers anyway. There wasn't a real lesson to be learned, but the intended lesson was to see how various animals act in their "natural" environment. I found that ironic because they were in a zoo, where they were bound by walls or fences and constantly bothered by people passing by and kids screaming.

Almington Academy had rented out the Central State Zoo for the day, so we had the entire place to explore for ourselves. "All right, everybody, listen up!" I heard Mr. Scott yell. "Each group has a piece of paper with questions. I want you all to write your names at the top, and there is no way for you to answer them without going to the exhibits. You can choose whatever time you want to leave, because I feel you're all responsible enough. The earliest bus is at 3:00pm, then 5:00pm and the last at 7:00pm."

Once he finished explaining, we entered the zoo at 11:30am. "Where do you guys wanna start?" Devin asked.

Travis responded; "well, I already planned how we could get through this paper in the shortest amount of time", further saying, "I doubt anyone here could care less about the paper as long as we get out in time for the 3:00pm bus".

Trevor responded, saying; "well, 'the paper' is two hundred points and twelve percent of your total first-quarter grade, so I'd suggest you care a little more." Trevor continued, "I think it's best we start at the Asia trail on the east side, head south, loop around the birdhouse, pass through the African walk and continue south through the rest of the zoo. We'll eventually loop up back to the entrance and cover the west side of the zoo." By the time he finished, we'd already begun the Asia trail.

First, was the panda enclosure. There were four Panda Bears in sight. When we tried to leave to the next enclosure, Trevor insisted we'd go inside. So, we tried to go in, only to hear that the mothers were nursing, so we couldn't see them. After walking for eight minutes and barely seeing animals, Travis came up to me and whispered, "hey, we're thinking about ditching Trevor. Are you with us or not?" I looked over to the other members of the group who were all looking at me anxiously, including Wyatt. Trevor was actively distracted by the orangutans he was mimicking.

"But he's your brother and I don't think it's the right thing to do. What if Mr. Scott finds out?" I said. I wasn't used to doing bad things, although this didn't seem that bad. I knew there was no way we could get out of this scot-free, until Travis told me his plan.

"Don't be like that. If we stay with him, we won't be leaving until the seven o'clock bus, and you know it. Here's the plan," he started, moving me away from the group a little bit. "He packed hand sanitizer because he thinks that public bathrooms only give you more germs. When we go to eat, we all go to the bathroom, and leave him," he explained.

"That doesn't account for Mr. Scott though. He'll definitely find out," I suggested.

"We'll tell him that we planned on leaving on the three o'clock bus and that we all agreed that if we got separated, we should all meet on the bus. When we couldn't find him on the bus and the bus started to leave, we called him multiple times, but the calls didn't go through as there was no signal. We just need to all have the same story," he added, pointing to the "No Signal" reading at the top left of his phone. I conformed, and he notified the group.

Wyatt walked up to me, looking troubled, and said, "look man, I don't wanna do it either, but I'm really tired, and it's way too hot to be here for another four and a half hours." I didn't respond because I heard Travis talking to Trevor.

"Hey, Trev, sorry about earlier," he started.

"You're sorry? Well, okay, I guess I don't know what to say," Trevor replied, a bit suspicious. Travis was a good speaker and evidently very convincing when he spoke. He was known for being able to talk himself out of any situation. He associated with

Keefe and Glenn, even though he was in the silver class, especially when they played pranks on teachers who had wronged them.

Travis picked up on Trevor's suspicion way too easily and provided a failsafe by saying, "the only reason I'm apologizing is because we're all hungry, and we can't be on bad terms and get you to agree to go and eat, since you're the leader of the group." By calling Trevor the leader, Travis empowered him to another level.

"Well, I guess we can grab something to eat around 2:00pm," Trevor said, insisting he didn't plan on leaving at 3:00pm. Travis agreed.

At 2:00pm, we arrived at the outdoor food court, where there were a few other groups, one including Mr. Scott, but he was too far away to notice anything. "Let's sit here. It's in the shade," Trevor insisted, gesturing at the most convenient seats in the court. It was perfect, but the seats were facing the restrooms, and we couldn't have that working against our plan.

We all looked at Travis, to which he said, "too many bugs." Trevor looked around the table skeptically, he eventually agreed to move to the table in the corner, backing the restrooms.

"Let's go wash our hands," Alex said.

We all began walking away, to sell the plan, I turned to Trevor and said, "aren't you coming?"

He shook his head and said, "studies show that

there are more germs on public bathroom door handles than those that were preexisting on your hands." Then he squirted a blob of sanitizer on his hands.

"Okay...?" I replied. We didn't even bother going into the bathroom because Trevor was completely oblivious. We ran down the path and looped around to the primates building.

"We did it!" Travis exclaimed.

"What're we gonna do for an hour?" Devin asked.

"I have it all figured out," Travis said. "The lion-feeding show starts at two and ends at 2:45pm. The enclosure is just ten minutes from the bus." We all smiled at how perfectly the plan was put together. We later made our way to the show, which was really cool.

Mr. Scott appeared near us. "This may or may not be a question on your paper," he said with a smile then walked away. That scared us all, but luckily, he didn't notice there were only five of us. Travis pulled out the map as a replica of the worksheet, because Mr. Scott decided to sit right next to us.

It then clicked that if it was a question, odds were that Trevor was going to be appearing soon. I notified Travis, but he was already thinking the same thing, he knew we couldn't leave in the middle of the show, without raising suspicion.

"I have a plan," Devin said. Devin wasn't a very dependable person, considering he'd gotten in trouble twelve times with academic dishonesty. "We just walk out, and if Mr. Scott asks later, we'll say that's when we realized Trevor was missing and went to look for him before going to the bus."

It wasn't a bad plan, especially since Mr. Scott would most likely take five people's words over Trevor's.

We left and when we turned toward the direction of the bus, I spotted Trevor and he spotted us. "Travis!" I yelled, pointing at Trevor.

"Run!" he shouted back. He was blocking the bus path, so we turned and ran back into the main zoo. He stayed on our tail for a while, but we lost him in the bamboo playground. We then sprinted to where the bus was parked. We could still hear Trevor screaming after us, but we got on the bus, all five of us, we did it!

Before the bus driver left, he began counting students. When he noticed that the number of students on the bus wasn't divisible by six, he told us that we couldn't leave until Mr. Scott was notified.

Travis the genius said, "Mr. Scott was in our group, but he said that he would stay until the last bus to make sure everyone is out of the zoo." The bus driver drank the Kool-Aid and drove off. All five of us felt good, our plan worked!

When we arrived back at school and the bus had left, we all cheered ourselves. Travis said one last thing before we left; "when Mr. Scott asks, we need to make sure that we all have the same story. You got that?" he said, mainly looking at Wyatt and me.

"Yeah," we both said.

As we disbanded, Wyatt said to me, "I'm gonna go catch up with Travis, Devin, and Alex. You can join us if you want."

"Nah, I'm winded, bro. I think I'm gonna go get some shut-eye," I lied.

"All right. See you later," Wyatt replied.

9

Caught in a web

In class Monday, the entire class went by without any suspicion. Trevor periodically looked over at me and sneered. I was a bit stressed out because it seemed like we were about to be in trouble, until the smallest gesture provided much-needed comfort to Wyatt and me.

Travis turned to us and winked, mouthing, "I got this. Let me do all the talking."

At the end of class, when we were walking to the elevator, Mr. Scott said, "Group Three, please stay back." That was our group, so we listened. Everyone seemed pretty chill with the situation, even Wyatt. I looked like the one who was going to crack under pressure.

I just hoped Mr. Scott wasn't picking up on that as much. Luckily, Mr. Scott wasn't all too familiar with Travis' reputation, so he was as trustworthy as anyone else in the room; except Devin of course.

It crossed my mind that Mr. Scott had probably spoken with the bus driver, so I began to sweat a little. Mr. Scott started with, "so, does anyone want to explain why you ditched Trevor?"

Then Travis put on the most convincing face, as we all furrowed our eyebrows. Travis replied with, "ditched? How did we ditch him? We spent almost the entire time there looking for him!"

Travis really sold it, so Trevor yelled, "Liar! They ran away from me when I found them!" Trevor tried to attack Travis. Mr. Scott got between them and asked us to explain.

Travis started with, "well, just to provide some background, we all agreed that if any of us got separated from the group, we should meet on the bus at 3:00pm".

Then Travis was interrupted when Trevor said, "he's lying again, Mr. Scott! Don't believe him!"

"Let him finish, or I'll kick you out," Mr. Scott replied assertively, while remaining calm.

"Thank you. Now, as I was saying before he butted

in, Mr. Scott, we went to grab something to eat, we all went to the bathroom to wash our hands, but he doesn't like washing his hands because he believes public bathrooms have too many germs.

When we came back out, he was gone, we walked around looking for him. There was only one chance to get the lion question done, so we stopped looking for him and went to the show where we saw you. When we realized that it's probably not safe for him to be out there alone because he could get lost, we left mid-show to search for him.

Shortly after, Devin reminded us that our meet-up spot was on the 3:00pm bus. We'd been looking for him for thirty minutes, so it was already 3:05pm. We had to run through half the zoo to the bus, when we got on, we didn't see him, the bus driver was already running late so, we ended up not being allowed to get back off. We tried calling you and Trevor, but there was no signal."

The story came out perfectly, we thought we had it in the bag, until Mr. Scott said, "well, the only question that your group didn't get was the eating habits of the lion." He was gesturing to the blank line.

Travis said, "when you handed out the worksheet, Trevor and I agreed that I'd hold the worksheet if he wrote the answers, and we'd help him with finding the answers. So, I held it until we went to go eat, which is when I wanted to give it to him to hold, but by then he was gone.

I forgot that happened because I still had the map in my back pocket. That's the reason we left the show before they even fed the lions. I would never leave my twin brother for any reason, Mr. Scott, you have to believe that." It was concerning how good Travis was at lying and how fast he'd come up with that part of the story.

"It checks out to me. Trevor, anything to add?"

"Yes, I have something to add! He's lying! That doesn't explain why they ran away from me."

"Well, you've earned yourself a detention. Next time you won't scream in my face. The reason they were probably running from you was because you were chasing them when they were going to the bus. I doubt they'd intentionally put themselves in this situation. You boys can leave. Trevor stay back, you might as well serve your detention now."

We all left without a word, except Travis who thanked Mr. Scott. I felt bad, but everyone else started laughing and mocking Trevor in the elevator, including Wyatt, which really shocked me.

When we got into the lobby, I asked Wyatt if he wanted to join the gang at Pancraziano's and he said, "sorry, bro, I already have plans with them," gesturing to his new friends that he'd just met on the field trip, just a few days ago.

When I got to Lockwood and met with Clyde, Ken, and Emily, I told them about the situation that occurred. "I'm thinking about coming clean. Trevor's stuck in there for hours and he's innocent. What do you guys think?" I asked.

Clyde started with, "hey, man, you gotta make your own choices. We can't make them for you. You know what's right and what's wrong. It's your choice on which one you'd like to execute. All I know is that whatever you do won't change the way I think about you."

Emily agreed, but what shocked me the most was Ken's reply, "bro, you have to come clean. He's innocent and you know it. I've been in situations like this numerous times, and they're all I'm able to think about. Obviously, mine are on a much larger scale, such as burning a whole floor of the library and blaming a bruin, but I would've taken the blame if I could."

"That was you? I thought it was Clarence!" Emily exclaimed.

Then Clyde added, "it's not too late to come clean. He's expelled, dude."

Ken added, "yeah, but why. It's already over. The past is the past. Don't tell anyone, by the way." We laughed a little. I finished my pizza and headed back to the Animal Science Building, to see Mr. Scott.

I walked into the classroom and said, "Mr. Scott, I'm sorry but everything Travis said is a lie. We ditched Trevor and ran away when he found us."

Mr. Scott looked dumbstruck and replied, "well, I

don't appreciate you guys lying and putting another groupmate in danger, but I do applaud your honesty. You can leave now; I'll think of a consequence for you and your accomplices.

Trevor, I'm sorry for not believing you," he said firmly.

Trevor and I rode down the elevator in silence. When we were walking out the door, he said to me, "what made you come back and tell the truth?"

I replied, "well, I have some pretty good friends and it's the right thing to do, I should have done it sooner." We parted ways, as he waited for the bus, I walked over to him and asked, "do you wanna join us at Lockwood?" He accepted gleefully. In the car, we watched some Love and Living Animals until we arrived at Lockwood.

"Guys, meet Trevor, Trevor, meet Emily, Clyde, and Ken." They greeted and accepted him, we sat down to go over the zoo ditching experience and laughed over it all.

Two days later after class, Mr. Scott held us all back again, including Trevor. Travis looked confident as always. This time, Wyatt shared the same confidence as he did, which disgusted me. "Well, Joey came clean about what actually happened, I was unable to decide a reasonable consequence, so I decided to let Trevor figure out each of your punishments, on top of the detentions you'll all be receiving, including Joey." I was content with that.

Trevor began; "well, since Travis is the only one

who lied through his teeth, his can be escalated to the administrative level." Travis's face went pale.

"Devin, Wyatt, and Alex can clean feces from the animal research facility every day for one week, I think Joey's okay with just a detention," Trevor stated with a wink.

"So be it. You can all serve your detentions now, Trevor, you can be on your way," Mr. Scott added.

After the detention, everyone left clearly pissed at me and swearing revenge, including Wyatt. He walked up to me and said, "I'm disappointed in you, Joey. I can't believe that you'd turn against your own friend like this. Especially for someone you just met, a few days ago. Now I'm gonna have to scoop feces for a whole week.

Next time you should think about how what you do affects others before doing it. I hate you." He left the group chat shortly after, but it was okay because I added Trevor in his place.

10

Building lasting bonds

Soon it was time for the parent-teacher conferences. My family came visiting, my mom, Elizabeth and Brad. It was great seeing them, I had missed them so much. I was not so hostile to Brad. Being at Almington Academy, making new friends, and the pleasant experienc had softened my view of him.

Days, weeks, months went by; school activities and study intensified, it became more challenging, P.E was gruesome and draining, the gang of Pancrazies & Clyde grew stronger in our friendship – the pinnacle, diamond, gold, silver or bronze tags and social classifications didn't matter within our gang of friends.

We were now, a group bound with the cord of friendship, looking out for each other's best interests.

The academic projects we worked on together, the exciting and fun times we shared, the sweat and tears of high school grind made us stronger together and individually.

It was a chilly night; we were all thinking about the coming spring break, Emily, Clyde, Ken, Trevor and I sat at Pancraziano's for some hot chocolate and pizza when Ken asked; "why didn't Travis ever get an administrative punishment?".

"Because they're all a bunch of robots!" I replied.

"You've been spending too much time with Mr. Theft", Emily quipped.

"Oh, are you guys ready for spring break?" Ken asked.

"Yeah, I got the road trip plans ready, hotels booked, cars ready, all set. It's gonna be quite the trip," Clyde replied with a genuine smile.

-The End-

Elkridge Elementary School – EES, laid the foundation for the realization of the book; Almington Academy. The long walk to getting this book to you started with well-paced steps as a 3rd grade student, tended and taught by a teacher who saw in him, what he did not see in himself, at the time.

Moroti Oyeyemi's love for reading and writing was stirred by his 3rd grade teacher, Ms. Sherri Sloat. She helped stimulate a talent that was seeded within him, with many after-school reading engagements, the desire to reach deep and unearth the treasure of creativity earnestly began. He developed his understanding and writing through reading and deep thoughts, often reflecting over all he read, rewriting and reimagining most in his mind.

Consequently, he began writing short stories, witty phrases and poems. His insatiable passion for reading is only paralleled by his innate drive to write. His writing style is unique, it's captivating and engaging. From his first sentence, he pulls his readers into his world, they become a willing and participatory audience in an ongoing and fast evolving scenery of events and drama.

He seeks to create in his audience a feeling of déjà vu – locating them right in the middle of the narrative, creating a sense of belonging, fellow travelers on an exciting and interactive journey. While Moroti pursues a degree in Software Engineering after high school in 2020, reading and writing will always be an undying passion. He has three books in the works and hopes Almington Academy is a good read for you.

69845299R00071

Made in the USA
Middletown, DE
22 September 2019